Richard Linche, Robert Lylesse

Diella

certaine sonnets

Richard Linche, Robert Lylesse

Diella

certaine sonnets

ISBN/EAN: 9783337848200

Printed in Europe, USA, Canada, Australia, Japan

Cover: Foto ©Andreas Hilbeck / pixelio.de

More available books at **www.hansebooks.com**

Diella: Certaine Sonnets.

Diella:

CERTAINE SONNETS.

BY

R. L. GENTLEMAN.

Ben balla, à chi fortuna suona.

AT LONDON.

Printed for *Henry Olney*, and are to be Sold at his
shop in Fleet-streete, neer the Middle-temple
Gate. 1596.

Edinburgh:
E. & G. GOLDSMID.

1887.

We certify that this Edition consists of TWO Copies VELLUM, and NINETY-SEVEN copies on paper. This copy is

No. 92

E. G. Goldsmid.

EDINBURGH, 23RD MAY, 1887

INTRODUCTION.

NO research has yet discovered the name of the
Author of these Sonnets.—A poem entitled
Being in Love he complaineth in the PARADICE OF
DAINTY DEVISES—bears a similar signature ; and
Barnefield in his "POEMS IN DIVERS HUMORS" 1598,
addresses the first Sonnet "To his friend Maister
R. L. in praise of Musique and Poetrie." It would
seem that Ritson had never seen the book, as he
states the number of Sonnets at twenty-eight instead
of thirty-eight. He appears to have derived his
information from Warton's History of English Poetry.
This error remained uncorrected in the new Edition
of that valuable work, probably from the same
cause.

The Lady Ann Glemnham to whom the Printer
dedicates the volume, was the eldest daughter of the
celebrated Thos. Sackville, afterwards Earl of Dorset.

TO THE MOST WORTHILY HONOURED,

AND VERTUOUS BEAUTIFIED LADY, THE

LADIE ANN GLEMNHAM, WIFE TO THE MOST

Noble, magnanimous, and woorthy

Knight, Sir Henry Glemnham, &c.

MADAM, Your many honourable vertues hauing
tyed mee to your eternal scruice, to shewe some part
of my dutie, I present your Ladiship with a fewe
passionate Sonnets,

Daine (gentle Lady) to accept them, and therein
shew the greatnesse of your benignitie, in receiving
curteouslie a gift of so smal worth, which though it
cannot any wayes equall eyther the number of your
vertues, or the greatnes of that noble house, whence
your Ladiship is discended, impute it not (Madam) to
my defect of Iudgement, but of Fortune : for were I
furnished with the greatest riches that blind Goddesse
could bestow on a man of my state, both they, and I
woulde fall prostrate at your feete, and euer rest at

Dedication.

your Ladiships deuotion : yet Madam as it is, it is a
chylde of the Muses, and therefore worthy to be
cherrished, conceiued in the braine of a gallant
Gentleman, and therefore to be fauoured ; sent into
the world by mee, who haue euer honoured your
Ladyshyp, and therefore craue of your Ladiship to bee
protected, to whom I ever wishe long life, lengthened
with all honorable happines.

Your Ladiships

in all dutie

Henry Olney.

SONNET I.

WHen first the feather'd God did strike my hart
　　with fatall and ymedicable wound,
　leaving behind the head of his fell dart,
　my bloodlesse body fell vnto the ground ;
And, when with shame I reinforc'd my might
　　boldly to gaze on her so heavenly face,
　huge flames of fire she darted from her light,
　which since have scorcht me in most pitious case:
To quench which heate, an Ocean of teares
　　have gushed out from forth my red-swolne eyes
　but deep-fetch'd sighs the raging flame vpreares,
　and blowes the sparkes vp to the purple skies.
Whereat the Gods afraid that heaven should burne,
Intreated Love that I for e're might mourne.

SONNET II.

SOone as the Azur-color'd Gates of th' East
 were set wide open by the watchful Morne,
 I walkt abroad (as having tooke no rest)
 (for nights are tedious to a man forlorne)
And viewing well each pearle-bedewed flower,
 then waxing dry by splendour of the sunne,
 all scarlet-hew'd I saw him gin to lower,
 and blush as though some haynous act were done.
At this amaz'd, I hy'de me home amaine,
 thinking that I his anger caused had :
 and at his set, abroad I walkt againe,
 when (loe) the moon lookt wondrous pale and
  sad.
Anger the one, and envie mov'd the other,
To see my loue more faire then Loues faire mother.

SONNET III.

SWift footed time, looke back and here mark well,
   those rare-shapt parts my pen shall now declare;
   my mistres snow-white skinne doth much excell
   the pure-soft woll arcadyan sheepe doe beare ;
Her hayre exceedes gold forc'd in smallest wire,
   in smaller threds then those *Arachne* spun ;
   her eyes are christall fountaines, yet dart fire
   more glorious to behold then Mid-day sun ;
Her Iuory front (though soft as purest silke)
   lookes like the table of Olympick *Ioue*,
   her cheekes are like ripe cherries layd in milke,
   her alablaster neck the throne of Loue ;
Her other parts so farre excell the rest,
That wanting words, they cannot be exprest.

SONNET IV.

WHat sugred termes, what all-perswading arte,
    what sweet mellifluous words, what wound-
       ing lookes
   loue vs'd for his admittance to my hart?
   such eloquence was neuer read in bookes :
He promis'd pleasure, rest, and endlesse ioy,
    fruition of the fairest shee aliue,
    his pleasure paine, rest trouble, ioy annoy,
    haue I since found, which me of blisse depriue.
The Trojan horse thus haue I now let in,
    wherein inclosed these armed men were plac'd,
    bright eyes, faire cheekes, sweet lips, and milk-
      white skin
   These foes my life have ouerthrown and raz'd.
Faire outward shewes, proue inwardly the worst,
Loue looketh faire, but Louers are accurst.

SONNET V.

THe little Archer viewing well my loue,
    stone-still amaz'd, admired such a sight,
    and swore he knew none such to dwell aboue,
    though many fair, none so conspicuous bright :
With that inrag'd (flamigerous as he is)
    he now gan loathe his *Psiches* louely face,
    and swore great othes to rob me of my blisse.
    saying that earth for her was too too base ;
But *Cytherea* checkt her lordly sonne,
    commaunding him to bring no giglet thether,
    fearing indeed, her amorous sports were done
    with hote-spur *Mars*, if hee should once but see
        her.
If then her beauty moue the Gods aboue,
Let all men judge if I haue cause to loue.

SONNET VI.

Mirror of beautie, natures fairest chyld,
 empresse of loue, my harts high-prized
  Iewell,
 learne of the Doue, to loue and to be milde,
 be not to him that honors thee so cruell :
But as the aspe, deafe, angry, nothing meeke
 thou wilt not listen to my dolefull plaint,
 nor once wilt looke on my discolored cheeke
 which wanting blood, causeth me oft to faint ;
Then silent will I be, if that will please thee,
 yet so, as in my stead, each Plaine, each Hill,
 shall echo forth my griefe, and thereby ease mee,
 for I myselfe of speaking haue my fill ;
If Plaines, and Hills, be silent in my paine,
My death shall speake, and tell what I sustaine.

SONNET VII.

WHen Loue had first besieg'd my harts strong
wal,
rampair'd and countermur'd with chastitie,
and had with Ordnance made his tops to fall,
stouping their glory to his surquedry,
I call'd a parley, and withall did craue
some composition, or some friendly peace ;
To this request, he his consent soon gaue
as seeming glad such cruell warrs should cease ;
I (nought mistrusting) opened all the gates,
yea, lodg'd him in the Pallace of my hart,
when (loe) in dead of night he seekes his mates,
and shewes each Traytor how to play his part ;
With that they fir'de my hart, and thence gan flie,
Their names, Sweet smiles, faire face and piercing Eye.

SONNET VIII.

Ike to a Faulcon watching for a flight,
　　duly attending his desired game,
　haue I oft watcht and markt to haue a sight,
　of thy faire face exceeding niggard Fame :
Thyne eyes (those lumynaries of my griefe)
　　haue been more gladsome to my tyred spright
　then naked sauadges receiue reliefe,
　　by comfort bringing warmth of *Phœbus* light ;
But when each part so glorious I had seene,
　　I trembled more then Autumnes parched leaues,
　mine eyes were greedy whirlepooles sucking in
　　that heauenly faire which me of rest bereaues :
Then as thy beauty thus hath conquered mee,
(Faire) let relenting pitty conquer thee.

SONNET IX.

B Lot not thy Beautie (fairest) yet vnkinde,
　　with cruell vsage of a yeelding hart,
　　the stoutest Captaine scornes such bloody minde,
　　then mingle mercy where thou causedst smart ;
Let him not die in his May-springing dayes,
　　that liuing vowes to honour thee for euer :
　　shine forth some pitty from thy sun-like rayes,
　　that hard froz'd hate may so dissolue and seuer ;
Oh, were thou not much harder then a flint,
　　thou hadst ere this been melted into loue,
　　in firmest stone small raine doth make a print,
　　but seas of teares cannot thy hardnes moue,
Then wretched I must die before my time,
Blasted and spoyled in my budding prime.

SONNET X.

WHen *Flora* vaunts her in her proude array
  clothing faire *Tellus* in a spangled gowne,
 when *Boreas* furie is exil'd away,
  and all the Welkin clear'd from cloudy frowne:
At that same time all Natures chyldren ioy,
  trees, leaues, flowers bud, plants spring, and
   beasts increase:
  only my soule, surcharg'd with deep annoy
  cannot reioyce, nor sighes, nor teares can cease:
Only the grafts of sorrow seeme to grow,
  set in my hart, no other spring I finde,
  delights and pleasures are o'regrowne with woe,
  laments and sobs possesse my weeping minde;
The frost of griefe so nyps Delight at roote,
No sunne but shee can doe it any boote.

SONNET XI.

WHat shee can be so cruell as my Loue
    or beare a hart so pittilesse as shee?
  whose loue, lookes, words, teares, prayers do not
    moue,
    nor sighes, nor vowes preuaile to pittie mee,
She calls my loue a *Synon* to her hart,
    my lookes (she saith) are lyke the Crocadyles,
    my words the Syrens sing with guilefull arte,
    teares *Cyrces* floods, sighes, vowes, deceitfull
      guiles :
But my poore hart hath no interpreter,
    but loue, lookes, words, teares, prayers, sighes or
    vowes,
    then must it die, sith shee my Comforter,
    what ere I doe, nor liketh, nor allowes.
With *Titius*, thus the vultur sorrow eats me,
With steele-twig'd rods thus tyrant *Cupid* beats mee.

SONNET XII.

THou (like the faire-faced Gold encouer'd booke
    whose lines are stuft with damned herisies)
dost in thy face beare a celestial looke,
when in thy hart liue hell-borne cruelties.
With poysenous Toades the clearest springs, infected,
    and purest Launes nought worth if full of staines:
so is faire beauty when true loue's reiected ;
    when cole-blacke hate within the hart remaines.
Then loue (my deere) let that be Methrydate
    to ouer-come the venome of disdaine ;
be pittifull, tread downe his killing hate,
    conuert to sugred pleasure, gall-full paine :
O, sith disdaine is foe vnto thy Faire,
Exile him thence, there let him not repaire.

SONNET XIII.

I Know, within my mouth for bashfull feare,
   and dread of your disdaine, my words wil die ;
  I know, I shall be striken dumbe (my deere)
  with doubt of your vnpittifull reply ;
I know, when as I shall before you lie
   prostrate and humble, crauing help of you,
   mistic aspects will cloude your sun-bright eye,
   and scornefull lookes oreshade your beauties
    hewe ;
I know, when I shall pleade my loue so true,
   so stainlesse, constant, loyall and vpright,
   my truthfull pleadings will not cause you rue ;
   the ne're heard state of my distressed plight.
I know, when I shall come with face bedight
With streaming teares faln from my fountaine eyes,

SONNET XIV.

BReathing forth sighes of most hart-breaking night
    my teares, my sighes, and me, you will despise:
    I know, when with the power that in me lyes,
    and all the prayers and vowes that women moue,
I shall in humblest mercy-mouing wise
    intreate, beseech, desyre, and beg your loue ;
    I know (sweet mayden) all will not remoue
    flynt harted rigour from your rocky breast,
But all my meanes, my sute, and what I proue,
    proues bad, and I must liue in all unrest.
Dying in life, and liuing still in death,
And yet nor die, nor drawe a life-like breath.

SONNET XV.

WHen broad-faced riuers turn vnto their foun-
      tains
   and hungary Wolues deuoured are by Sheep,
   when marine Dolphins play on snow-tipt Moun-
      tains,
   and foule-form'd Beares do in the Ocean keep :
Then shall I leaue to loue, and cease to burne
   in these hot flames wherein I now delight ;
   but this I knowe, the Riuers ne're returne,
   nor silly Sheep with rauening Wolues dare fight,
Nor Dolphins leaue the Seas, nor beares the woods,
   for Nature bids them all to keepe their kinde ;
   then eyes, rayne forth your ouer-swelled floods,
   till drowned in such Seas may make you blind :
Then (harts delight) sith I must loue thee euer,
Loue me againe, and let thy loue perseuer.

SONNET XVI.

NO sooner leaues *Hyperion Thetis* bed,
   and mounts his coach to post from thence away,
  richly adorning faire *Leucotheas* head,
  gyuing to mountaynes tincture from his ray:
But straight I rise, where I could find no rest,
  where visions and fantasies appeare,
  and when with small adoo my body's drest,
  abroad I walke to thinke vpon my deere;
Where vnder vmbrage of some aged Tree,
  with Lute in hand I sit and (sighing) say:
  sweet Groues tell forth with Eccho what you see,
  good Trees beare witnes who is my decay,
And thou my soule, speake, speake what rest I haue,
When each our ioyes dispayre doth make me raue.

SONNET XVII.

BUt thou deere sweet sounding Lute be still,
   repose thy troubled strings upon this mosse,
   thou has full often cas'd me gainst my will,
   lye down in peace, thy spoile were my great losse.
Ile speake inough of her (too cruell) hart,
   enough to mooue the stonie Rocks to ruth,
   and cause these trees wepe tears to heare my
      smart,
   though (cruell she) will not once way my truth.
Her face is of the purest white and red,
   her eyes are christall, and her haire is gold,
   the world for shape with garlands crown her head;
   and yet a Tygresse hart dwells in this mold ;
But I must loue her (Tigresse) too too much,
Forc'd must I loue, because I find none such.

SONNET XVIII.

THe sun-scorcht Seaman when he sees the Seas
    all in furie hoist him to the skye,
    and throwe him down againe (as waues do
      please)
    (so chased clouds from *Eols* mastiues flye)
In such distresse prouideth with great speede
    all meanes to saue him from the tempests rage,
    hee showes his wit in such lyke time of neede,
    the big swolne billowes furie to asswage;
But foolish I, although I see my death,
    and feele her proud disdayne too feelinglie,
    which me of all felicitie bereaueth,
    yet seeke no meanes t'escape this miserie;
So am I charm'd with hart-inchaunting beautie,
That still to waile I thinke it is my dutie.

CUpid had done some heynous act or other,
    that caus'd *Isala* whip him very sore ;
    the stubborne Boy away runs from his Mother,
    protesting stoutly to returne no more ;
By chance I met him, who desir'd reliefe,
    and crau'd that I some lodging would him giue :
    pittying his lookes which seemed drown'd in
        griefe,
    I tooke him home there thinking hee should liue;
But see the Boy ; envying at my lyfe,
    which neuer sorrow, neuer loue had tasted,
    he rays'd within my hart such vncouth strife,
    that with the same my body now is wasted,
By thanklesse Loue ; thus vilely am I used,
By using kindnes, I am thus abused.

SONNET XX.

WHen night returnes backe to his vgly mantion,
    and clear-fac'd morning makes her bright
      vp-rise,
    in sorrowes depth, I murmer out this caution:
    (salt teares distilling from my dewy eyes)
O thou deceitful *Somnus* God of Dreames,
    cease to afflict my ouer-pained spright
    with vayne illusions, and idle Theames,
    thy spells are false, thou canst not charm aright;
For when in bed I thinke t'imbrace my loue
    (inchaunted by the magique so to thinke)
    vaine are my thoughts, 'tis empty ayre I proue,
    that still I waile, till watching make me winke:
And when I winke I wish I nere might wake
But sleeping carryed to the *Stigian* Lake.

SONNET XXI.

THe strongest Pyne that Queene *Feronia* hath,
    growing within her woody Empire,
    is soon throwne downe by *Boreas* windy wrath,
    if one roote only his supporter be ;
The tallest Ship that cuts the angry Waue,
    and plows the Seas of Saturnes second sunne,
    if but one anchor for a iourney haue,
    when that is lost gainst euery Rocke doth runne;
I am that Pyne (faire loue) that Ship am I,
    and thou that anchor art and roote to me :
    if then thou faile (oh faile not) I must die
    and pyne away in endlesse miserie ;
But wordes preuaile not, nor can sighes deuise
To mooue thy hart, if bent to tyrannize.

SONNET XXII.

AS winters rage young plants vnkindly spilleth,
  as haile greene Corne, and lightning floures
    perish,
  so mans decay is loue, whose hart it killeth,
  if in his soule hee carefully it cherish;
O how alluringly hee offers grace,
  and breathes new hope of lyfe into our thought,
  with cheereful, pleasant (yet deceitfull) face,
  he creepes and fawnes, till in his net w' are caught,
Then when he sees us Captiues by him led,
  and sees vs prostrate humbly crauing helpe,
  so fierce a Lyon *Lybia* neuer bred,
  nor Adders sting, nor any Tigresse whelpe :
Oh blest be they that neuer felt his force,
Loue hath nor pitty, mercy, nor remorse.

SONNET XXIII.

Looke as a Bird, through sweetnes of the call
    doth cleane forget the fowlers guilefull trap ;
    or one that gazing on the Starres doth fall
    in some deepe pit bewayling his mishap ;
So wretched I, whilst with *Lynceus* eyes,
    I greedily beheld her angels face,
    was straight intangled with such subtilties,
    as euer since I liue in wofull case ;
Her cheekes were Roses, layd in christall glasse,
    her breastes two apples of *Hesperides*,
    her voyce more sweete then famous Thamiras,
    reuiuing death with dorique melodies ;
I harkning so to this attractiue call,
Was caught, and euer since haue liued in thrall.

SONNET XXIV.

M Y lyues preseruer, hope of my harts blisse,
    when shall I know the doome of life or
      death?
    hell's fearefull torments easier are then this
    soule's agonie, wherein I now doe breath:
If thou would'st looke, this my teare-stayned face
    dreery, and wan, far differing from it was,
    would well reueale my most tormentful case,
    and shew thy faire, my griefe as in a glasse;
Looke as a Deere late wounded very sore
    among the Heard full heauely dooth feede,
    so do I lyue; expecting euermore
    when as my wounded hart should cease to bleed:
How patient then would I endure the smart,
Of pitchy-countnanc'd Deaths dead doing dart.

SONNET XXV.

WHen leaden-harted sleep had shut mine eyes,
    and close oredrawn their windolets of light,
    whose watrynes the fire of grief so dries,
    that weep they could no longer, sleep they might ;
Mee thought, I sunke downe to a poole of grief,
    and then (me thought) such sinking much did
        please me,
    but when I down was plung'd past all reliefe,
    with flood filled mouth I call'd that some would
        ease me ;
Whereat (me thought) I saw my deerest loue,
    (fearing my drowning) reach her hand to mine,
    who pull'd so hard to get me vp abouc,
    that with the pull sleep did forsake myne eyne :
But when awakt I sawe twas but a dreame,
I wisht t'had slept and perisht in that streeme.

SONNET XXVI.

Rough stormes haue calmes, lopt boughes do grow
  agayne,
  the naked winter is recloth'd by spring,
  no yeare so drie, but there doth fall some raine,
  nature is kind (saue me) to euery thing.
Onely my griefes do neuer end nor cease,
  no ebbe doth follow my still-flowing teares,
  my sighes, are stormes which neuer can appease
  their furious blastes procur'd by endlesse cares ;
Then sighes and sobs, tell *Tantalus* he's blest,
  goe fly to *Titius* tell him hee hath pleasure,
  so tell *Ixion* though his wheele ne're rest,
  their paines are sports imposed with some
    measure ;
Bid them be patient, bid them looke on me,
And they shall see the Map of miserie.

SONNET XXVII.

THe loue-hurt hart which Tyrant *Cupid* wounds,
    proudly insulting o're his conquer'd pray,
doth bleede afresh where pleasure most abounds,
for mirth and mourning always make a fray.
Looke as a Bird sore bruzed with a blowe,
    (lately deuiding notes most sweetly singing)
to heare her fellowes how in tunes they flowe,
doth droope and pine as though her knel were
    ringing.
The heauie-thoughted Prys'ner full of doubt,
    dolefully sitting in a close-bar'd cage,
is halfe contented, till he looketh out,
    he sees each free, then stormes hee in a rage;
The sight of pleasure trebleth euery payne,
As small Brooks swell and are inrag'd with rayne.

SONNET XXVIII.

THe heauens Herrald may not make compare
    of waking words which so abounds in thee,
  thy hony-dewed tongue exceedes his far,
  in sweete discourse, and tuneful mellodie ;
Th' amber-color'd tresse which *Berenice*
    for her true-louing *Phtolomeus* vow'd,
  within *Idalias* sacred Aphrodice,
  is worth-lesse with thy lockes to be allow'd :
To thee my thoughts are confecrate (deere loue)
    my words and phrases bound to please thine eare,
  my lookes are such as any hart could moue,
  I still sollicit thee with sighes and teares ;
O let not hate eclypse thy beauties shine,
Then none would deeme thee earthly, but deuine.

SONNET XXIX.

WEarie with scruing where I nought could get,
  I thought to crosse great *Neptunes* greatest Seas,
  to lyue in exile ; but my drift was let,
  by cruell Fortune spitefull of such case ;
The Ship I had to pass in, was my minde,
  greedie desire was topsaile of the same,
  my teares were surges, sighes did scrue for winde,
  of all my Ship dispayre was chiefest frame ;
Sorrow was maister, care the cable rope,
  griefe was the maine Mast, Loue the Captaine of it,
  he that did rule the helme, was foolish hope,
  but beautie was the Rocke that my Ship split :
Which since hath made such shipwreck of my ioy,
That still I swim in th' Ocean of annoy.

SONNET XXX.

CEase eyes to cherrish with still-flowing teares,
    the almost witherd rootes of dying griefe,
  dry vp your running Brooks, and dam your meares,
  and let my body die for moist reliefe ;
But death is deaffe, for well he knowes my paine,
  my slakelesse payne hells horror doth exceede,
  there is no hell so blacke as her disdaine,
  whence care, sighes, sorrowes, & all griefes do
        breed ;
In steede of sleep (when day incloistred is
  in dustie pryson of infernall night)
  with broad-wakt eyes I waile my miseries,
  and if I winke, I feare some vgly sight ;
Such fearefull dreames do haunt my troubled mind,
My Loue's the cause, cause shee is so vnkind.

SONNET XXXI.

H E that can count the candles of the skie,
  reckon the sands whereon *Pactolus* flowes,
or number nomberlesse small attomie,
 what strange and hideous monsters *Nilus* shewes,
What mishapt Beasts vast *Affrica* doth yield,
 what rare-form'd fishes lyue in th' Ocean,
 what colour'd flowers doe grow in *Tempes* field,
 how many houses are since the world began :
Let him, none else, gyue iudgement of my griefe,
 let him declare the beauties of my Loue,
 and hee will say my paines pass all reliefe,
 and hee will iudge her for a Saint aboue ;
But as those things ther's no man can unfolde,
So, nor her faire, nor my griefe may be tolde.

SONNET XXXII.

FAire iuorie browe, the bord Loue banquets on,
    sweete lyps of Corrall hue, but silken softnes,
faire Sunnes that shine when *Phœbus* eyes are gon,
sweet breath that breaths incomparable sweetnes :
Faire cheekes of purest Roses red and white,
    sweet tongue, contayning sweeter thing then
        sweet ;
    O that my muse could mount a loftie flight,
    and were not all so forcelesse and vnmeete,
To blaze the beautie of thy seuerall shine,
    and tell the sweetness of thy sondry tast,
    able of none but of the Muses nine,
    to be arightly honored and grac'd ;
The first so faire, so bright, so purely precious,
The last so sweete, so balmy, so delicious.

SONNET XXXIII.

THe last so sweet, so balmy, so delicious,
　　lips, breath and tongue, which I delight to
　　drinke on,
　the first so faire, so bright, so purely precious,
　brow, eyes and checks, which still I ioy to thinke
　　on :
But much more ioy to gaze, and aye to looke on
　those lilly rounds which ceaseles holde their
　　mouing
　　from where my prisoned eyes would nere begon,
　which to such beauties are exceeding louing ;
O that I might but presse theyr dainty swelling
　and thence depart to which must now be hidden,
　and which my crimson verse obtaines from telling,
　because by chast cares I am so forbidden ;
There in the christall-paued vale of pleasure ;
Lies locked vp a world of richest treasure.

SONNET XXXIV.

THinking to close my ouer-watched eyes,
　　and stop the sluce of their vncessant flowing,
I layd me down when each one gan to rise,
　(new-risen *Sol* his flame-like count'nance shewing)
But griefe, though drowsie euer, yet neuer sleeps,
　　but still admits fresh entercourse of thought,
　duly the passage of each houre he keepes,
　　nor would he suffer me with sleepe be caught ;
Some broken slumbers *Morpheus* had lent,
　who greatly pittied my want of rest,
　whereat my hart a thousand thanks him sent,
　and vow'd to serue him he was ready prest :
Let restlesse nights, daies, howres doe their spight,
Ile loue her still, and loue for me shall fight.

SONNET XXXV.

WHy should a Maydens hart be of that proofe,
    as to resist the sharpe-point'd darte of
loue ?
    my Mistres eye kills strongest man aloofe,
    mee thinks he's weak that cannot quaile a Doue.
A louely Doue, so faire and so diuine,
    able to make what *Cynick* so e're liueth,
    vpon his knees to beg of her bright eyne
    one smiling looke, which life from death reuiueth ;
The frozen hart of cold *Zenocrates*,
    had beene dissolued into hot desire,
    had *Phryne* cast such sun-beames from her eyes,
    (such eyes are cause that my hart flames in fire)
And yet with patience I must take my woe,
In that my dearest loue will haue it so.

F

SONNET XXXVI.

ENd thys enchauntment (Loue) of my desires,
    let me no longer languish for thy loue,
  ioy not to see mee thus consume in fires,
  but let my cruell paines thy hard hart moue :
And now at last, with pittifull regard,
    eye me thy Louer, lorne for lacke of thee,
  which dying liues in hope of sweet reward,
  which hate hath hetherto with-held from me ;
Constant haue I been, still in fancie fast,
    ordayn'd by heauens to dote vpon thy faire,
  nor will I e're, so long as life shall last,
  say any's fairer, breathing vitall ayre :
But when the oceans sands shall lye unwet,
Then shall my soule to loue thee (deere) forget.

SONNET XXXVII.

LOng did I wish before I could attaine
    the lookt for sight I so desir'd to see,
  too soone at last I saw what bred my baine,
  and euer since hath sore tormented mee ;
I saw herselfe, whom had I neuer scene,
    my wealth of blisse had not been turn'd to baile :
    greedy regard of her, my harts sole Queene,
    hath chang'd my summers sun to winters haile.
How oft haue I since that first fatall houre,
    beheld her all-faire shape with begging eye,
    till shee (vnkind) hath kil'd me with a lowre,
    and bad my humble-suing lookes, looke by.
O pitty mee (faire Loue) and highest fame
Shall blazed be in honour of thy name.

SONNET XXXVIII.

Id I not loue her as a Louer ought,
  with purest zeale and faithfulnes of hart,
then she had cause to set my loue at nought,
and I had well deseru'd to feele this smart :
But holding her so deerely as I doe,
  as a rare Iewell of most high esteeme,
shee most vnkindly wounds and kills me so,
  my nere stain'd loue most causeles to misdeeme ;
Neuer did one account of woman more
  than I of her, nor euer woman yet
respected lesse, or held in lesser store,
  her Louers vowes, then shee by mine doth set.
What resteth then, but I dispaire and die,
That so my death may glut her ruthlesse eye.

SONNET XXXIX.

Harken awhile (Diella) to a storie,
    that tells of beautie, loue, and great dis-
  daine,
  the last, caus'd by suspect ; but shee was sorry,
  that tooke that cause, true loue so much to paine ;
For when she knew his faith to be vnfained,
    spotles, sincere, most true, and pure vnto her,
    she ioy'd as if a kingdome shee had gained,
    and lou'd him now as when he first did woo her.
I nere incur'd suspition of my truth,
    (fairest Diella) why wilt thou be cruell ?
    impose some end to vndeserued ruth,
    and learne by others how to quench hates fuell.
Reade all, my Deere, but chiefly marke the end,
And be to mee, as shee to him, a friend.